DINO WARS
The Gladiator Games

DAN METCALF

illustrated by **Aaron Blecha**

To BRIZAUL

REXTOPIA

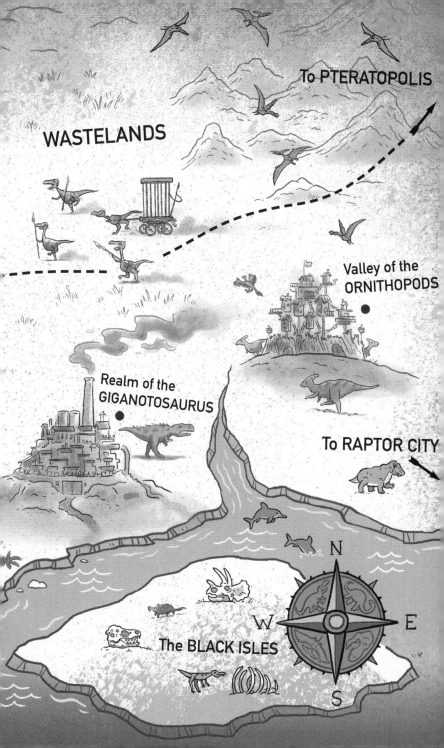

Chapter One.

"En garde!" shouted Oska. He held his staff aloft, standing side-on to Adam. "Prepare to meet thy maker!"

"Ha! No chance, old man!" said Adam, arming himself with a heavy stick from the ground. "I mean, old... dino?"

They were in a dense, green forest, where Dag still lay in his cleverly constructed hammock. The rest of their group had slept on the ground and got up an hour before, but Dag had not tried to get up yet; it has often been said that there is no graceful way to get out of a hammock, and that was doubly true for a huge iguanodon. Two curly-haired twins, Tuppence and Benji, sped around the temporary camp that the group had set up, playing 'it' with their four tiny lycorhinus friends. Chloe, Adam's sister, muttered to herself as she tried to clear up their mess and pack away the camp. She threw water on the campfire, making a hiss followed by a column of steam. Meanwhile, S'Ariah, the newest addition to their travelling party, hung upside-down from a branch, calling instructions to Adam,

"Adam, feet shoulder-width apart. Left arm out to the side to counter-balance the weight of your sword – or stick, in this case."

"How do you know so much about combat?" asked Oska, the elderly oviraptor.

"Essential training for pterosaurs," she said. "You?"

"Oska fought in the Dino Wars," said Adam. "Come on, show me your best moves!"

"Pah! Moves? I will show you strikes and

parries of the highest order," said Oska. "If you can see them, that is – I was the fastest swordsman in the Raptor Army!" He waved his staff around in the air as if to prove his point, the swishing sound echoing through the forest. Adam grinned, tired of waiting for the duel to commence.

"ATTACK!" he yelled, running at Oska with his stick held high. Oska easily stepped to one side, flipped Adam's weapon out of his hand with his staff, and kicked him up the bottom as he passed. Adam fell face-first into the dry mud of the forest floor.

"If you want to gain the element of surprise, try to not shout your next move as you launch into it," suggested S'Ariah.

She let go of the branch and spread her wings, which allowed her to float down gently like blossom on a spring wind. She landed less gracefully, plonking down on the make-shift tent that Benji and Tuppence had slept in. It collapsed under her weight. "Oops! Oh well, I've taken the tent down for you!"

Chloe finally looked up from her frantic tidying.

"I don't know how you've got time to stand around and play-fight!" she said. She stuffed some food scraps into a bag and carried on clearing up. "We're only halfway through our mission and the fate of the world is at stake!"

Adam got to his feet, brushing himself down. He hated it when his little sister moaned at him, but today it was a welcome distraction after just getting his bottom kicked by an ageing raptor.

"Chill Chlo'!" he said. She never liked being called 'Chlo' and he knew it. "For a start, we're *training*, not 'playing'. Oska offered to teach me some basic hand-to-hand combat. It might come in useful, especially as we're entering T-Rex territory soon!"

"What?" called Dag. He sat up in a panic and

upset his delicate balance in the hammock. It span around and he tumbled out, thumping down onto the ground.

"I thought we were going to go *around* Rextopia? I'm sure there are plenty of crystals in the Valley of the Ornithopods?"

"We *will* go around it," Adam reassured his best friend. "I'm not stupid enough to walk into a city of tyrannosaurs! I was learning a few moves just in case we come across a rogue hunter. And anyway, Chloe, we're way more than halfway through the mission. We've got three Dilotron crystals! We only need four!"

Chloe threw down the bag she was packing.

"We still need to make it to Brizaul and disarm the huge virus weapon-thingy!" she said. "I just don't think we should be larking about with pretend swords when all the dinosaurs on New Earth are in danger."

"MUM!"

"RIGHT!"

"LET'S!"

"GO!" said the little lycorhinuses in turn. Although she was touched that they agreed, she was baffled by their name for her.

"Wait, *I'm* your mum now?" she said. Her eyebrows knitted together in a frown that only ever came out in moments of high confusion or annoyance. "Why just me? Why not Adam? Or the twins?"

"MUM!" said Hart.

"FEED!" said Karp.

"MUM!" said Trek.

"SAFE!" said Grak.

"You should be flattered, Chloe!" said Benji.

Chloe sighed. How come she was the only one cleaning up after everyone and making sure they ate? She was only ten years old after all! She looked around the camp where the twins were still running amuck, playing with the lycorhinuses. Adam continued his training. Oska was easily beating him, even with one of his claws behind his back and his eyes closed. Looking down at the pile of rubbish she had been clearing up, Chloe kicked it over and grabbed a nearby stick from the forest floor.

"I want to fight!" she announced, striding over.

"I'm not sure that's wise, young Chloe," said Oska. "I was ranked a 'master' in fencing at the academy, you know. I wouldn't want to accidentally hurt you!"

Chloe smirked and turned her back on Oska.

"Oh, I won't be fighting you, Oska," she said. "I'm fighting Adam."

Adam laughed. He raised his weapon and stood with his feet apart like S'Ariah had told him.

"Excellent!" he smiled. "May the best man win!"

"I will!" said Chloe. While she was hot-headed enough to walk into a sparring match with her brother, she soon realised that she didn't have a clue what to do. She looked at the long, thin stick. It was easily twice her size.

"Ah, you chose a staff as your weapon? Marvellous!" said S'Ariah, appearing by her side to offer advice. Chloe hadn't meant to (or even known it was called a staff), but nodded along. S'Ariah corrected her posture and told her where to put her hands. "Defend against strikes like this," said S'Ariah, miming a sword fight in front of her, "and attack like this!" She thrust her imaginary staff up and down, as though she was miming a wood cutter with a nasty grudge against a tree.

"Okay," said Chloe. "When do I…?"

"ATTAAAACK!" yelled Adam, running at her. His war-cry had given Chloe enough time to get into her defending stance and she blocked the strike from above. She turned to face him as he ran past, looking for an opportunity to get him back. She was worried about how seriously he was taking it. She held the staff out, the point aimed at Adam's chest, and ran at him.

He easily deflected her blow, bashing his stick into hers. Her staff fell to the floor, taking her with it. She turned and saw Adam about to bring his heavy, blunt stick down on her, and managed to lift her staff across her chest, blocking his strike. Adam stepped back and prepared to strike again. Chloe leapt to her feet.

"I say, well done Chloe!" cheered Oska. "Whatever you do, don't lose concentration!"

"Huh?" said Chloe, momentarily turning her attention to Oska. Adam chose that exact moment to strike at her. Luckily, her staff was at the right angle to protect her body but she was unprepared – Adam's hefty stick came down hard on hers and snapped it in two!

"HEY!" she yelled. Adam regained his footing and placed the tip of his 'sword' onto her chest.

"Victory is mine, I think?" he said smugly.

Chloe looked at the two halves of her staff. She bashed him away with one half and leapt to her feet.

"Never!" she yelled.

"Chloe, be careful!" said S'Ariah. "We don't want to let anger get the better of us, now do we?"

"Aaaaagh!" shouted Chloe, ignoring her friend. She ran towards Adam, her arms swinging with two pieces of staff in her hands, like a lethal windmill. The blows came raining down on her brother –

SLAM! CLASH! BANG! SMASH!

Adam managed to block most of them with his weapon. He staggered back and tripped, landing on his bum.

"I submit!" he yelled. Chloe stopped immediately and dropped her weapons, out of breath.

"Well, that was certainly… um… energetic?"

said S'Ariah. "But you shouldn't let anger get the better of you, Chloe."

Chloe walked away, still seething. Adam stood up again and brushed himself off.

"Normally I'd agree," he said. "But Chloe fights so much better when she's angry. We used to play-fight all the time back in Bastion. But if I got her angry? Well, then we weren't playing anymore..."

*

Chloe returned to gathering up her camping supplies. Dag stood nearby, rolling up his hammock.

"You alright?" he said. Chloe sighed and shrugged.

"I just... I want to be taken seriously, you know? And Adam drives me so mad sometimes!" she said. She could confide in Dag. They had known each other since they were babies and there was nothing they couldn't share. "I mean, what am I even here for, apart from playing 'mum' and cleaning up after you lot? If I'm not making a difference to the quest, I might as well go home. Sometimes I feel that all I'm good for is reading the map."

Dag was about to utter a few words of encouragement, but Benji and Tuppence came running through the camp, bashing into the pile of rubbish Chloe had just collected. Garbage flew up and was caught by a breeze, spreading it far across the forest.

"Oops!" said Tuppence. "Sorry!"

"OI!" cried Chloe. "Clean that up NOW!"

Benji and Tuppence froze, sensing the anger in Chloe's voice.

"Alright, keep your hair on!" said Benji.

"Yeah!" called Tuppence. "Don't get so upset about a load of rubbish Chlo'!"

"So are you coming or what?" asked Benji. "'Cos we need you to read the map."

Dag looked at Chloe, who was red with what was either rage or embarrassment. Whatever it was, he felt the need to take her bag and pack it for her.

"Come on," he whispered in what was meant to be a calming way. "Let's get moving. Maybe we'll even meet a nice carnivore who can take the twins off our hands?"

Chapter Two.

Adam and Dag emerged from the woodland.

"Yikes!" said Dag. He looked out across the flat, barren landscape of the scrublands. "It's so... vast!"

Adam could only nod. The area they stood in had once been acres of lush green land with rolling hills and hedgerows, littered with villages and hamlets. People had lived there; real, live humans. It had stayed that way for years until the wars came. First there were the Gene Wars which ripped families and cities apart. They flattened the land and burnt all the trees. When it became clear that neither army of humans would succeed, a genius named Lucius Green created a weapon that would help his side win the war.

Dinosaurs.

Genetically engineered to speak and think tactically, they were the ultimate weapon – at least they *were*, until they rebelled. Then the Dino Wars began and the once lush, green fields became battlefields again.

"Nothing has grown in this soil for years," said Dag, picking up some of the dry, white soil and crumbling it in his claws.

"Not since we lost the Dino Wars," said Adam. His gaze fogged over, lost in thought. His father had fought on those fields. And Oska's relatives, and S'Ariah's. His father may have even fought against the very species Adam was now travelling with!

There was not a person on the planet the war had not touched but now they were the only ones left; the few remaining humans had settled in

Bastion,
Adam's home, along with
some peaceful herbivore dinosaurs.

He felt proud of how far they had come: they'd gone from fighting each other to working together.

"Stop standing about!" called Benji's voice as he climbed out of the undergrowth. "Which way to the crystals?"

Adam snapped out of his daydream and waited for Chloe, S'Ariah, Tuppence and Oska to join them.

"Chloe, the map please!" said Adam, holding out his hand like he was a surgeon asking for a scalpel and a damp sponge. Chloe gritted her teeth and passed him the rolled up map, smashing it into

his stomach. "Oof! Ah, thank you."

He unfurled the map on the dry mud floor and looked at it, turning his head from side to side and trying to match it up with the cities that he could see, far away on the horizon. One of the cities seemed to be belching out smoke from an industrial chimney. Another was smaller, seemingly protected from the outside world by a rudimentary wall made of bamboo and twigs. The last was enclosed in a white stone wall, flags flying from each corner.

"Where to, boss?" asked Tuppence. Adam continued to stare at the map, befuddled.

"It's no good," he muttered. "This map is

broken," he said. He looked up with a frown and an 'ah-well' shrug.

Chloe bent down and turned the map upside-down, until the points on the map reflected the cities on the horizon.

"Ah! Yes! I was… just, um, testing…" spluttered Adam. Chloe covered her mouth to stop herself from laughing while Dag bit on his claw. The others found something interesting to look at in the nearby wildlife (of which there was none). Adam did his best to carry on.

"So, going east to west, we have the Valley of the Ornithopods–" He pointed to the simple bamboo-walled settlement, "–then the Realm of the Giganotosaurus–" He pointed to the industrial chimney. "Or Rextopia," he said, gesturing to the high stone walls.

"The question is: which do we fancy our chances with?" asked Chloe.

The team looked at each other.

"Well, the T-Rex place sounds a bit bitey-bitey," said Benji.

"And the Giganotosaurus place sounds a tad stompy-stompy?" chanced Dag.

"Ornithopods it is then!" said Adam. He clapped and rubbed his hands together. "A nice, friendly species. Should be a walk in the park."

"Finally!" said Chloe. "I don't know about you, but I don't fancy any quest, challenges or trials again any time soon."

"Exactly!" said Adam, laughing. "And thank goodness we don't have to meet any T-Rexes! I mean, I like an adventure, but I like my head too!"

The group laughed and prepared to set off again. Chloe, for one, found it refreshing that they were going to try requesting a crystal from a friendly species of herbivore for once. Maybe she could use politeness and flattery to ask for the crystal? Maybe she could be of use after all?

They were just about to take the first footstep of many towards the Valley of the Ornithopods, when a loud rumbling sound piped up. It was deep, like an avalanche of rocks falling down a mountainside. Adam and Chloe exchanged worried looks.

"Dag, is that your tummy?" asked Oska.

"Not this time," said Dag. "S'Ariah, can you get an aerial view?"

The clumsy pterosaur nodded and spread her wings, unfurling her massive wingspan. She took a few steps and caught the wind, rising up quickly and swooping in circles until she found a thermal to hover on.

"Anything?" shouted Chloe. S'Ariah started to shout, but she was too far up for the team to hear. "What? Come lower!"

S'Ariah closed her wings, causing her to plummet towards the ground. She spread them again at the last second to slow her descent like a

parachute.
She landed next
to Adam.

"I said: 'TROODONS! RUN!'"

Chloe looked up and saw a cloud of dust coming closer and closer. In the centre was a herd of troodons, two-legged dinosaurs with claws that rip and jaws that bite. There were twenty or so, each galloping at full speed towards them. Some towed cages on trailers behind them, some ran with spears. They only seemed to have two pulse blasters between them, but that was more than enough weaponry to cause some serious damage.

"Split up!" yelled Adam. "Back into the woods!"

They turned but before they could even reach the edge of the forest, ten grinning troodons emerged from the undergrowth. Adam skidded to a halt.

"Oska, you're an old soldier," he said, backing away and keeping his eyes on the troodons coming from the forest. "What would you do in this situation?"

"You mean, with thirty armed enemy fighters surrounding us in a pincer movement?" asked Oska. "Only one thing to be done, old chap. Surrender."

He hated to do it, but Oska was right. Slowly, Adam raised his hands above his head and nodded for the rest to do the same.

"Freeze!" came a yell from the heart of the troodon group. "Put 'em up!" The troodons parted and one stepped forwards. He was no bigger than the rest of the group, but he commanded an air of authority. He had a scar on one side of his face and wore what looked to be a leather waistcoat and something on his head.

"Is that... a *cowboy* hat?" whispered Dag to Adam. Peering closer, Adam saw that it was indeed a small Stetson hat. As the troodon was only waist-high to an adult human it must have originally been a child's dressing-up hat, which made it look slightly comical.

"Howdy   partners!" said   the   Stetson'd troodon. "Name's Klint. Y'all are trespassing on troodon land."

"Troodon land? We had no idea you had a territory!" said Adam. "No harm meant; we'll be on our way!"

Adam turned to walk away but one of the smaller dinosaurs stepped forward, growling and pointing a spear straight at Adam's nose.

"Or we can stay right here!" said Dag. He erupted into nervous laughter. When no one joined in, he added in a small voice: "Please don't eat us."

"Ha!" said Oska. "No fear there! Troodons aren't really the killing kind. Unless you're a weak little hatchling or an egg in a nest!"

"Takes one to know one, *oviraptor*," said Klint. He stepped closer, walking amongst the group, paying particular attention to Chloe and Tuppence. He looked them up and down, sizing them up. He smiled and nodded appreciatively. "Heck, I ain't seen a human in years! Least of all a female! Where you been hidin'?"

"Please, we're on an important mission," said Adam. "We have to get to Brizaul to save the lives of every dinosaur on the planet!"

Klint burst into laughter.

"Hear that, boys? The *human* is gonna save us!" he called to the surrounding troodons. They laughed too, a cackle and a roar of dinosaur voices. "How about that? After years of trying to destroy us, now they want to take us under their wing! Ain't that sweet?"

Oska spoke up.

"If it were a lie, would I be with them?" he called. The laughter died down.

"Or me?" said Dag.

"Or me?" said S'Ariah. "I was sent by the elders of Pteratopolis to ensure they carried out their mission."

The troodons fell silent. If their dinosaur companions were speaking for them, then perhaps the story was true? Klint squared up to Adam, staring him in the eye, his snout almost touching his nose.

"Is that so?" he whispered in a menacing tone. Then he immediately backed off. "Okay!"

Adam lowered his arms cautiously.

"Really? We can carry on our mission?"

he asked. "We're free to go?"

Klint nodded and tipped his hat to them.

"Well... kinda," he shrugged. He let out an ear-piercing whistle and suddenly the troodons were creeping closer. There was a strange sound – a *thwoop, thwoop, thwoop,* of something being swung through the air. Chloe looked up and screamed as several troodons swung lassos over their heads. They threw the ropes and each landed easily on one of their group. They pulled tight and Adam and Benji felt the rope tighten around them, their arms pinned to their sides. Dag, with his strong dinosaur arms, was able to break free instantly but the troodons quickly lassoed him again, three ropes landing on him this time and pulling tight.

"Hey!" screamed Tuppence. "Get off me!"

"Klint?" called Adam. "You said we could go!"

Klint leant casually against a wagon which held a strong cage. He held out his claws in an apology.

"Sorry, man!" he said. "You can carry on your merry way, but I got these here critters to feed." He pointed at the hungry troodons around them, salivating as they tied each of them up. "You still trespassed, and I can't let that go. So here's the deal. I take your females, you go and complete your mission thing. Can't say fairer than that!"

"WHAT?" yelled Dag. "You'd better hope these ropes are unbreakable, 'cos there is no WAY I am letting you walk away from here to go and eat my friends!"

Klint nodded and the troodons holding the ropes pulled hard, making Dag groan. He stepped forward and stroked Dag's cheek.

"Shush now, big fella!" he said. "We ain't gonna eat 'em! We're gonna sell 'em!"

"Pardon me?" said S'Ariah. "I'm not a piece of meat, you know!"

"Not yet," grinned Klint. "Nah, I'm just

messin' with ya! Y'all are gonna be stars! You'll be sold to the Gladiator Games!"

There was a few seconds of silence. Then Adam laughed.

"But… they're girls!"

"Hey!" shouted Chloe, before realising that he was just trying to talk them out of taking them. "I mean, yeah! What would they want with me?"

Klint leapt up on top of a cage.

"Are you kiddin' me? In Rextopia, all gladiators are girls! It's their tradition – the guys sit around all day while the gals go huntin'. You know, like lions?"

The troodon pack tied each one of them and carried Chloe, Tuppence and S'Ariah into waiting cages.

"But… I'm a kid!" protested Tuppence.

"A *human* kid!" said Klint. "I bet those T-Rexes will pay top dollar for human gladiators. And a flying dino too! Rextopia is desperate for more slaves to fight. They're putting on a huge competition with a big prize for anyone who can defeat the grand champion, and I want me some of that show business money!"

"You won't get away with this!" called Adam. It would have sounded much more threatening if he wasn't tied up, face down on the ground and surrounded by thirty dinosaurs.

"Sorry pal," said Klint. "I think I just did!"

With another ear-piercing whistle, the troodons ran off as one, the wagons clattering along the uneven ground. Adam struggled to pull his head up, and was just able to see Chloe in her cage as she disappeared from view.

"I'll find you, Chloe!" he yelled. "I'll rescue you!"

Chapter Three.

Adam, Dag, Benji and Oska lay in the dirt, their arms tied behind their backs.

"Well, this is a mess isn't it?" said Oska.

Adam writhed and wriggled on the ground, attempting to loosen his ties, but the troodons had done a good job. They were out in the open too, so if they didn't get to shelter soon, the hot midday sun would fry them like an egg. Then, if they didn't manage to drink, they would die of thirst.

"I wouldn't say that, Oska," said Benji. He was remarkably calm for someone who had just seen his sister and friends carted away. "There's always a bright side."

"What's that, then?" said Dag. "We may all be tied up, but at least we have a lot of the troodons' rope?"

Benji grinned smugly.

"Except... we're not all tied up are we?" he said. He lifted his head as much as he could and gave a yell. "Hey, you guys!"

There was a rustle in the leaves of the nearby forest and Dag swivelled to look. Out of the undergrowth ran the four little lycorhinuses.

"What on New Earth?" said Adam. "Where have you been?"

"TROODON!"
"BAD!"
"WE!"
"HIDE!" they said in turn.

"Hmm. That was actually a very wise move," said Oska. "I say, you couldn't peck my ropes free, could you chaps? Lying like this is killing my back..."

Karp, Hart, Grak and Trek each leapt onto the back of their friends and pecked at the ropes with their beaks. They had freed them in a few minutes.

"I have never been so pleased to see you little blighters!" said Dag, rubbing Grak's head fondly.

"Is everyone okay?" asked Adam. "Dag? Oska? Benji?" He looked around. "Benji?"

Benji had climbed on top of a nearby rock.

"I can see the troodons! Wow, they're fast!" he called down. "Bad news, boys. Klint wasn't kidding - they're headed towards Rextopia!"

"That makes sense," said Oska. "Troodons are built for speed, and they'll want to sell their stock as soon as possible so they can buy food."

Adam kicked up a clod of mud.

"Can we not refer to my sister and friends as 'stock'?" he said.

"Like it or not, that's what they are to them,"

said Oska. "Slavery is very big in Rextopia."

Adam kicked the ground again, angry at himself. He could have done more; stopped Klint, gone after them, taken a different route. But now Chloe and the girls were gone.

"There's nothing you could've done," said Dag, reading his mind. "They were fast. They came out of nowhere."

Adam nodded but deep inside he was burning, blaming himself. Benji dropped to the ground from the rock and walked onwards.

"Where are you going?" asked Oska.

"That way!" said Benji, pointing to the cloud of dust on the horizon that had been kicked up by the army of troodons. "I'm going to get my sister back!"

"Benji! Wait!" called Adam. "Even if we do get to Rextopia, it'll take a day. Then what? It's a city full of the most feared carnivores in history! How would we, a pair of despised humans and a bunch of dinos, get through the city gates?"

They were silent for a minute, each trying to take stock of what had just happened. Oska looked down at the ground, where the remaining rope lay from the ties they had escaped. He pondered on them for a moment, then looked up at Adam, Dag and Benji. His raptor face spread into a large grin.

"Hang on, lads. I've got a great idea!"

43

*

The wagons rattled and clattered, kicking up dust and bouncing Chloe, Tuppence and S'Ariah up and down in their cage like a flea on a ferret.

"When I get out of here I'm going to roast you alive!" snarled Tuppence. "I'm going to drizzle you in barbecue sauce and serve you in a bun with a side-salad!"

The troodons around her pulling the wagons laughed, which only spurred Tuppence on to make even more ludicrous and unbelievable threats. "I'm going to deep fry you in oil and serve you with chips!"

Chloe, meanwhile, was silent. She was shaking in her tiny corner of the cage, but thankfully no one could see because the wagons were bouncing so much from being driven so fast. She looked out at the troodons and the approaching city with its white, stone walls.

She was scared. There was no point fooling

herself otherwise. She was frightened and she did not know what was going to happen. Her brother was gone and she was far, far from home.

S'Ariah, meanwhile, stayed characteristically optimistic.

"Don't worry, girls. I have a feeling everything's going to turn out alright!" she smiled. Both Chloe and Tuppence turned to eyeball her with disbelief.

The wagons slowed as they got closer to the city walls. They pulled to a stop outside the main gates and Chloe pressed her ears up against the bars until she could hear Klint talking to the guards on the gate.

"Hey there, big guy? How are ya? How's your momma? Say, is that a new tattoo? Anyhow, I got some prime stock in the cages back there and I got an appointment with you-know-who... Hmm? My papers? You know me, dontcha? I'm here all the time! Hmm? What's that? Okay, the last time we came through a few of my boys *may* have got into a bar-room brawl, but there'll be no trouble this time, no sir! Maybe if I leave my buddies out here while I take the stock and do the transaction? How about if I grease your claw with a few gold coins, here? Ah, thank you kindly, sir!"

And so, the rest of the troodons stayed outside the city while Klint unloaded the girls from their wagon and led them through the gates, tied by their hands and linked to each other by a long rope. As they passed, Chloe got a look at the guard that had just let them through.

She had never seen a real tyrannosaurus rex before, and he was enormous. Seriously huge. If the three of them had balanced on each other's shoulders, they still wouldn't have been as tall as the hulking T-Rex guarding the gate. He had scales with tattoos and wore leather armour and a helmet to protect his tiny brain. A fully-charged pulse blaster hung around his shoulders.

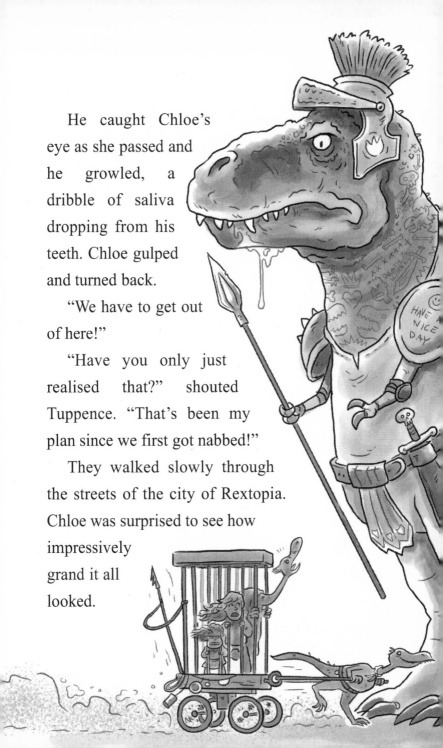

He caught Chloe's eye as she passed and he growled, a dribble of saliva dropping from his teeth. Chloe gulped and turned back.

"We have to get out of here!"

"Have you only just realised that?" shouted Tuppence. "That's been my plan since we first got nabbed!"

They walked slowly through the streets of the city of Rextopia. Chloe was surprised to see how impressively grand it all looked.

Wide avenues, buildings with white marble pillars and mosaics decorating the roads. It was a clean, sun-kissed place that she would have been glad to have visited. If it wasn't for the scary, armoured T-Rexes walking about and staring at them with curiosity, that is.

They came to a market square in the centre of the city and Klint stopped. He took off his hat and mopped his brow.

He used a sharp claw to cut their ropes.

"You're letting us go?" said Chloe, jumping down from the wagon.

"No, ma'am!" Klint laughed. "I just need you looking presentable for the buyer. You can run away if you wish, but remind yourself that you're in a city full of T-Rexes."

Chloe sighed while Klint attached a long line of rope to their hands like a dog's leash.

"Well, well, well!" came a voice from behind. "If it ain't my favourite thief and ne'er-do-well!"

Klint turned to see a magnificent ornithomimus with a shock of multi-coloured feathers. She was like a cross between a dinosaur, a peacock and a rainbow.

"GAMES MASTER!" roared Klint, and the two ran to each other and hugged. "It's been too long!"

"I assumed you'd been put in jail!" said the ornithomimus. "Wait! Business first. What do you have for me?"

Klint led her by the claw to Chloe, bent down low, like he was presenting a crown to royalty.

"As you can see, we have some very interesting finds here today, including not one, but TWO genuine humans," he said, showing them off.

"Marvellous, darling!" said the Games Master. "We haven't seen a human defeated in the ring since the end of the war!"

"Hey!" said Tuppence. "You haven't seen my moves yet!"

The Games Master flounced over to her.

"It speaks!" she said, shocked. "You know, my dear, we had all our human gladiators' voice boxes surgically removed after the war. It was very peaceful but the crowd complained that they couldn't hear them scream when they fought. Still, it's a sacrifice I'm willing to make again."

Tuppence gulped and shut her mouth.

The Games Master and Klint stepped away to

talk money. They spoke for a long time and eventually Klint came away with a heavy-looking bag and a smile on his face.

"Pleasure doing business with you," said Klint. The Games Master took the piece of rope that he had tied to each of their hands, like she was taking a houseful of dogs for a walk.

"Hmm. I wish I could say the same," she said. "You drive a hard bargain, Klint. Be careful no one follows you and steals your money on your way out!"

"Huh?" said Klint. "Is that a strange T-Rex saying?"

"No," said the Games Master. She led the girls away and waved goodbye, leaving a confused Klint in the middle of the market square. As he left, the Games Master whistled and two T-Rexes with muscles like mountains walked slowly after him.

The flashy ornithomimus led them through the

streets, past food stalls and art galleries, a T-Rex string quartet playing classical music and some tyrannosaurs waiting in line for the opera.

"It's all very, um… civilised, isn't it?" said S'Ariah.

"What were you expecting?" said the Games Master. "Carnage and chaos?"

"Well, yes, actually," said Chloe. "I must admit that I didn't have T-Rexes down as being so... advanced!"

"Ha! Honesty! I love it!" said the Games Master. "When I first came here it was a dump, but the new king has really turned it around. He found something to control the masses – something they love even more than fresh meat."

"What's that?" asked Chloe, although she was not sure she wanted to know the answer. The Games Master turned a corner and the girls looked up. Rising above them was the biggest structure Chloe had ever seen, even bigger than Stryker's tower back in Raptor City. It was an arena, built with columns of stone like those that Chloe had seen in books about Ancient Rome. It rose up, up, up above the streets and a banner was strapped to the outside with the Games Master's toothy grin painted over it. It read:

'The Games Master Presents...
The Most Amazing, Awe-Inspiring
Spectacle in Rextopia!
The Eighth Wonder of the World!
The Incandescent, Infamous,
Indescribable...
GLADIATOR GAMES!'

"That, my dear," said the Games Master, staring lovingly at her own picture, "was *entertainment!*"

Chapter Four.

The cells below the arena were dark and dank as Chloe had expected, but she hadn't counted on the *smell*. She lost count of the amount of cells as she was led past them, but each one contained a dinosaur of some sort and a bucket for their toilet. The stench was overwhelming.

"This is show business?" S'Ariah muttered.

The Games Master led them to an empty cell and beckoned them in. They shuffled forwards and looked nervously at each other. The Games Master stepped into the cell and produced a sharp knife from her belt. It was long and thin, with a bone handle. *Human* bone, if Chloe had to guess…

"Agh!" screamed S'Ariah. "No! Please don't torture us! We'll tell you everything we know!"

The Games Master reached out to cut Chloe's rope, freeing her. Chloe rubbed her wrists, thankful to have feeling in her fingers again.

"Torture?" laughed the Games Master. "Why would I want to torture my esteemed guests? My star fighters? No! You, my girls, will be treated like princesses."

She freed Tuppence and S'Ariah, then stepped outside and closed the barred door of the cell.

"Ah, that explains the 'palace-like' iron bars and the 'royal' bucket in the corner," said Chloe. The Games Master tutted and laughed.

"I know, it's awful isn't it? I apologise for the accommodation, but it's all we have. I'll send down some food – you must be *starving*, poor things. I hope your night is comfortable – you begin training at dawn."

She started to leave, but Tuppence leapt forward, grabbing at her through the bars and getting a hold on one of her lush turquoise feathers.

"Think it's going to be that easy?" Tuppence said. "Think these bars are enough to keep us in here?"

The Games Master, cool as a summer breeze, shrugged off Tuppence's grip.

"Keep you in, darling?" she smirked. "Oh no. The bars are there to keep your cell mates out."

She nodded to the next cell and walked away.

Chloe, Tuppence and S'Ariah slowly turned their heads to look at their next-door neighbour through the bars. It was an enormous T-Rex, grey in colour and almost filling the tiny cell. Her small eyes turned to her new neighbours.

"Oh, hello!" said S'Ariah in a friendly tone. "We're new here. I'm S'Ariah, this is–"

"I don't care!" barked the T-Rex. She stomped

sideways to get a better look at them. "If you're new, you only need to know a few things. One: if you wake me up, I'll bite your arm off. Two: if you eat loudly, I'll bite your other arm off. Three: we're not friends. If I come up against you in a show, you're going down. Now shut up: I'm going to sleep."

The T-Rex collapsed down on the floor and fell asleep almost instantly. The girls stood stock still, afraid to move in case they woke her up.

"DIN-DINS!" came a call. A small, feeble-looking dilophosaurus fiddled with some keys and unlocked their door, clanging the bars loudly.

"SHHHHH!" said Tuppence. "The troll will wake up!"
The dilophosaurus laughed.

"What, Leena? No chance!" he said, placing down three trays of food on the floor. "She could sleep through a war. Some say she did! I'm Hex, by the way."

Chloe breathed a sigh of relief and picked up the tray. She expected to see a bowl of gruel, but instead she had steamed vegetables with white rice, followed by a chocolate mousse and a summer berry smoothie.

"Wow! The food is better here than back home!" Chloe said. The door was now closed but they slipped the trays back through the bars.

"So it should be!" said Hex. "You're the Games Master's big attraction. She's got big things planned for you, y'know!"

Chloe actually found herself blushing.

"Gosh! Really?"

"Yeah, of course!" the dilophosaurus said, turning to leave. "No one's seen a human slaughtered since the war. They'll be queuing around the block!"

Chloe sat down in the corner, cuddling into her friends. Suddenly, she didn't feel so special after all.

*

"Rise and shine, ladies!" called the Games Master. "It's a brand new day in Rextopia and it's time for rehearsals!"

Chloe woke to find Tuppence's foot in her face. They had snuggled down together to get some sleep in the night but she'd tossed and turned so much that it was like sleeping in the same bed as a swarm of wasps. It had been cold on the floor of the cell, but S'Ariah had draped her wing over them all to provide a cover and they had all swiftly fallen asleep. They rose and found their cell door open. They cautiously peeked out into the corridor. Luckily, Leena the T-Rex had already left.

"Rehearsals?" questioned Tuppence.

"She means training," said a voice from down the corridor. It was Hex, the weak-looking dilophosaurus who was mopping the floors. "You have to train for the Gladiator Games."

"What happens if we don't train?" asked Chloe.

"Oh, that's easy; you lose your battle, and you die. If you want to get out of here, you've got to fight your way out!"

They followed the corridor until it brought them into the centre of the arena. A cluster of gladiators stood in the middle of the sand and sawdust ground. They were a motley bunch; an assortment of dinosaur species forced into slavery, from ankylosaurs to raptors, none of whom looked pleased to be there. The seats, empty for the moment, rose up around them. When full, it must have held thousands of tyrannosaurs, all cheering and baying for blood.

"Good morning gladiators!" said the Games

Master in a sing-song voice.

They shuffled closer to the group, purposefully steering away from Leena. She seemed even larger out in the open air, perhaps because she wasn't stuffed into a tiny cell. She was already dressed in metal armour, a helmet and carrying a large broadsword.

"Go on. Arm yourselves!" said the Games Master. She nodded to a cart full of weapons and armour that Hex had wheeled into the arena. There were swords, maces, spears, shields, slings and whips, plus an assortment of ill-fitting armour. Chloe and Tuppence grabbed whatever would fit, while S'Ariah grabbed a helmet that barely stayed on her head.

When it came to weapons, S'Ariah picked a sling, while Tuppence grabbed the mean-looking (and surprisingly heavy) mace. Chloe took the only weapon she had any experience with – a staff.

"Psst!" hissed Tuppence. She walked up beside S'Ariah. "How come you're still here? You could spread your wings and fly at any time! You could go and get help!"

S'Ariah looked shocked at the suggestion.

"Absolutely not! I wouldn't dream of abandoning my new friends! Well, my only friends, really..." she said.

Chloe overheard and whispered a quiet '*aww!*'. Tuppence shook her head, dismayed.

"Oh, and there's the small issue of *that*..."

S'Ariah pointed upwards. Chloe and Tuppence looked up to see a huge net stretched over the open-topped arena and a guard stood on the roof with a menacing looking pulse-blaster.

"Ah, yes," said Chloe. "Probably best you stay with us then."

The Games Master led the warm-ups; Chloe and Tuppence faired well. They were very fit after all the time spent walking on their quest. They mastered the sit-ups, squats and press-ups (which Leena failed to do with her tiny arms), while the star-jumps were made slightly problematic when S'Ariah tried them, and knocked over half the row with her huge wingspan.

"Excellent!" said the Games Master. "You – slightly larger human! You can demonstrate your fighting ability first."

The amassed gladiators stepped back to the edge of the arena, leaving Chloe in the middle, feeling tiny and scared.

"Um, when you say *ability*, I'm not sure I have any," she said with a nervous laugh.

"Nonsense, darling!" cooed the Games Master. She approached and put a comforting claw around her shoulder. "That's the stage fright talking. Now let's bash that away just like we bash in the brains of our competitors, hmm?"

"Um... right," said Chloe, not reassured in the slightest.

The Games Master picked a sparring partner for Chloe; it was a maniraptor, dressed in what looked like a medieval knight's armour and holding a wooden club.

"Positions!" called the Games Master. "And... ACTION!"

Chloe approached and decided to try and strike first. She threw the staff to her left but the maniraptor blocked it with the club. Chloe countered with a strike to the right leg, but her arms were so weak that she only tapped the armour, which rang like a dinner bell.

The maniraptor ran at her with the club raised and Chloe managed to block it with her staff – *yes!* But her opponent was fast and struck again, this time breaking the staff in two.

"Not again!" Chloe cried. The maniraptor ran at her, but Chloe knew just what to do.

She ran away. The crowd around her laughed as the maniraptor gave chase.

"Alright! Fight over!" the Games Master bellowed. Chloe and the rest of the gladiators moved back to the centre, where S'Ariah smiled supportively.

"Well done!" she said. "I mean, not great, but for a first go? You smashed it!"

"Really?" said Tuppence, confused. "From where I was watching, she got owned!" S'Ariah plunged one of her pointy elbows into Tuppence's side. "Ow! What did you do that for? Oh, I see. Yeah, great fight, Chloe!"

Chloe kept her head down.

"Hmm, I must say I'm disappointed," said the Games Master, noting down something on a clipboard. "But no matter! You will still serve a very important role in tonight's performance!"

Chloe looked up, hoping her 'important role' would be as a stagehand, or working the lights.

"You, my dear, will be the first on stage to warm up the crowd," the Games Master said. "Yes, you will be an 'easy kill' to whet the audience's appetite for the evening to come. What do you say to that?"

Chloe felt the energy drain from her body.

"Um... thank you?"

*

Outside Rextopia, in the wilds of the scrublands, two human boys and an iguanodon were being led by an elderly oviraptor. Tied by their hands, a rope around their wrists formed them into a chain gang. The dinosaur leading them approached the city gates of Rextopia.

"Good morrow, my noble friend!" he called as he came closer to the guard. The T-Rex stood and turned on his pulse blaster, which buzzed with energy. He swung it around to point at Oska.

"Who goes there? Friend or foe?" barked the guard.

"Friend! Friend!" called Oska, putting his claws in the air. "Just a travelling slave trader! The name's Oska. How do you do?"

The guard, obviously unimpressed by pleasantries, glared at Oska with a scowl of hatred.

"Never mind, let's skip that part, shall we?" said Oska. "I wondered if I could enter the city and sell these wretched souls?" He pointed to Adam, Dag and Benji, who played the part of tired, tied-up slaves very well.

"You got humans?" said the guard. He stomped over to inspect Adam, pulling open his mouth to check his teeth and prodding him with his pulse blaster.

"Indeed! A rare sight nowadays, wouldn't you say?" said Oska. "I bet you haven't seen a human in years, have you?" He was fishing for information. Luckily, the guard was more than happy to bite.

"Nah. Saw some yesterday. They were slaves n'all!"

Good, thought Adam. That meant the troodons brought Chloe and Tuppence to Rextopia, just as they thought, and S'Ariah would hopefully have been with them.

"Did you really?" said Oska, acting surprised. "What a coincidence. So may we pass?"

The guard looked Oska up and down.

"They well tied up? Wouldn't want them escaping, would you?" he grunted.

"These imbeciles? They wouldn't have the brain power! Look, barely a thought in their

71

heads!" Oska demonstrated by slapping Adam and Benji around the head. They winced but kept silent, playing their part. Oska went to do the same to Dag, but Dag shot back a look that said 'Don't push it.' Oska stepped back. The guard laughed.

"In you go. Try the market square to sell them," he said. "But I'll warn you. You won't get much for scrawny runts like those!"

Once through the gates, they found a deserted side street and Oska snipped the ropes off their wrists.

"You were enjoying that a little too much, Oska," said Adam, rubbing the back of his head.

"It got us in, didn't it?" he replied. "I always thought I'd

be good on the stage..."

Dag wriggled until Grak, the tiny lycorhinus, dropped out of his shirt where he'd been hiding like a dove up a magician's sleeve.

"SMELL!" said Grak, then let out a call that let the other lycos know that it was safe to come out of their hiding places. Trek, Karp and Hart dropped out of Oska, Adam and Benji's shirts, each looking ruffled and disgusted.

"UGH!"

"STINK!"

"BAD!" they said in turn.

"What did you expect?" said Benji. "We've been on the road for ages without a bath. It was never going to be spring-fresh in there!"

They stuck to the back alleys as

they wandered through Rextopia. The main streets were full of terrifying T-Rexes and they didn't fancy taking their chances.

"So we're looking for somewhere they would keep gladiators," said Benji. "What are we going to do about getting a crystal?"

"Yeah, we've not got much time. Around two weeks until the Coda Program goes off," said Dag. Adam shook his head.

"Let's concentrate on getting the girls back first," he said. "Goodness knows what sort of trouble they're in."

They moved around from back alley to back alley, freezing anytime they saw a T-Rex. Finally, they sat down on a few sacks of rubbish.

"Man, I am *beat!*" said Adam. "It's been hours and we still have no idea where they are."

Dag rested his claws and pulled a piece of litter off his foot.

"Hey, Adam?" he said. "Wouldn't it be great if

we could free the girls *and* get a crystal?"

Adam laughed.

"Well, of course it would! But what are the chances of that happening?" he said. He turned to Dag suspiciously. "Why do you say that?"

Dag held out the piece of litter he had pulled off his foot. It was a multi-coloured leaflet, emblazoned with the face of a grinning ornithomimus holding a familiar-looking green rock. It read:

Tonight! Join the Games Master for
The Gladiator Challenge!
Who will beat the Grand Champion?
Who will win their freedom **AND** the
Emerald Gem?
Find out at **THE GLADIATOR GAMES!**

"Because that is exactly what we're going to do!" said Dag.

Chapter Five.

The boys made their way through the back alleys of Rextopia. While the main streets were clean and modern-looking, the back streets showed the city to be scrappily built and bolted together much like the other dino-cities they had visited. It was like taking a peek behind the curtain and seeing how the magic trick was really done. It was also where all the other species of dinosaurs hung about. T-Rexes were the only ones allowed to roam the main streets, while traders and slaves like rogue raptors and gallimimuses scuttled about in the shadows.

It was also the home to lots of stalls, laid out

along the sides of the alleys. This was the market that no tyrannosaur would be seen dead at. The stalls sold nick-nacks, old tech, black market meat and some very obviously stolen goods. Adam saw swords for sale, fake shirts for the Gladiator Games, and antiques from the Dino Wars.

Dag could not be stopped from browsing an old tech stall, where he lovingly looked at pieces of old equipment.

"Adam, look!" he said, holding up a small black box. "This is a remote control! Humans used to use them when they were bored and needed entertainment."

"Cool," said Adam. "How?"

"Dunno," said Dag. "Maybe they juggled with them or something. Ooh, look, a cheese grater!"

Adam moved on to the next stall, which seemed to be selling bits of old junk. Old copper kettles and ancient tin cans sat alongside stuffed badgers and real, rare, paper books. Adam was about to pass by when he saw something glinting at him from the back of the table. He reached over and picked up a round disc. It was metal, dull and faded, but a quick polish revealed it to be a pendant, holding a familiar looking crest.

"Dag!" called Adam. "Is this what I think it is?"

Dag held a magnifying glass from his pocket up to his eye. He traced over the crest with a claw.

"A dinosaur… standing with… a human?" he said. "That's the crest of Bastion! But… that's impossible!"

"It's the same as Tora's necklace!" said Adam. He held it next to the large necklace that he wore as a belt. "When Tora gave this to me, she told me my mum had made it. Maybe she made both of them?

Dag nodded.

"But… how did it get from Bastion to here? No one had ever left Bastion before us…"

he muttered. "Or so we thought."

"You like?" said the stallholder, an old and wrinkled neovenator. "To you, just fifty gold coins!"

They were, of course, penniless. Oska tried to talk to the old vendor, but the canny dinosaur would not speak about how he got the pendant, insisting that 'information costs money, dunnit?' Reluctantly, Adam placed the pendant down. He vowed to return, but he knew that he had to press on with the small matter of finding and freeing his sister and friends.

The group walked and walked until they found the arena, rising high above them.

"Woah!" said Dag. "How did we miss that?"

Queues were starting to form around the arena for that evening's Gladiator Games. The tyrannosaurs from around the city were lined up waiting to get in. One or two T-Rexes looked over to them with some confusion – they hadn't seen a human since the Wars. Oska made a show of bashing them around the head again and shouting, to keep up the guise of being a slave trader.

"Get in line, you deplorable specimens!" he yelled. "Slaves for sale! Anyone take these disgusting humans off me for a price?"

"Hey, I'm not a human!" said Dag.

"I'll throw in the iguanodon for free!" shouted Oska.

"We need to get inside," said Dag. "But the arena won't let us in without a ticket."

"Yeah, what if the girls have to fight as gladiators?" said Adam. "I can't see Chloe lasting long against an opponent!"

"Hmm. Tuppence on the other hand would tear them apart," nodded Benji.

Just as Adam had formulated a plan to scale the outside of the arena and leap in over the top, they heard a deep, growling voice from behind them.

"YOU!"

Oska turned to see a huge T-Rex male looming over him. His scales were brown and his rows of hundreds of teeth were sharper than a velociraptor's claw. He wore a pale yellow shirt with the name 'Kyle' sewn on to it.

"Um… yes, my good man?" said Oska, trying to crack a smile even though he was shaking with fear. He only managed a grimace.

"You got slaves?" said Kyle.

"Hmm? Oh, yes?" said Oska. "Are you buying?"

Kyle unhooked a bag of gold coins from his belt and thrust it into Oska's claw.

"There. You won't get a better price for 'em," said Kyle.

"Well, of course!" said Oska, beaming. Adam caught his eye and shook his head. This was *not* part of the plan! "What do you need them for?"

Kyle pointed his stubby arms over at the arena.

"It's gonna be a big fight tonight. The Games Master's got human females in the ring!" he said. "I'll need all the help I can get."

Adam and Dag exchanged anxious glances.

"Doing what?"

Kyle gave a sinister laugh.

"You'll see!"

*

In the cells underneath the arena, Chloe sat on the floor, as still as a statue.

"Well, this is it. I always wondered how I would go," she said. "Turns out it'll be in front of ten thousand cheering T-Rexes."

"It's not *certain* that you'll die!" said S'Ariah. She was polishing the armour that she had chosen until it came up to a bright shine. "I mean, you never know what sort of opponent you could be fighting! Think positive, that's what I always say!"

Chloe looked over at S'Ariah who grinned happily, and it was impossible not to follow her lead. Even in the darkest of times, S'Ariah's positivity shone through the gloom.

"Yeah!" said Tuppence. "You go out and show them what humans are made of!"

The cell next to them was empty – Leena had remained up on the arena floor to train some more.

"How come she gets more training?" said Tuppence. "And food?"

"She's the champion," came a call. Two cells away, a triceratops was sitting on her floor. "People come to see the games to see how she'll stomp her next opponent. The Games Master gives her extra training so that she won't lose. If she loses, ticket sales drop."

"So if someone beats Leena, what do they get?" asked Tuppence.

"The top prize!" said the triceratops. "Freedom, plus the Emerald Gem."

Chloe let the words sit in her head for a moment until they made sense. Then she leapt up.

"Emerald Gem?" she said. "This big? Kind of see-through? Glowy?" The triceratops nodded. "YES!" Chloe punched the air.

"You think it's a crystal?" said S'Ariah.

"It has to be!" Chloe said. She was suddenly animated again. She had snapped out of her stunned silence and was thinking over what this meant. "The crystal is in this arena, probably with the Games Master herself."

"She keeps it in her office, locked up," the triceratops interjected.

"So if we can beat Leena in the grand fight, we could take the crystal, leave Rextopia and find Adam and the boys," said S'Ariah. "Yes! I love it when a plan comes together!"

The three girls high-fived each other. Their spirits were only slightly dampened by the fact that they were still in a cell under a gladiator arena.

"Of course, there's still the problem of having to fight Leena," Tuppence pointed out.

"And getting past my first fight," said Chloe, glumly. Even S'Ariah had a hard time trying to put a positive light on that situation. Chloe paced the cell for a few minutes until she arrived at a plan. "Of course! I've got it! What's the one thing the Games Master loves more than anything else?"

"Um… funky hats?" offered Tuppence.

"Dinos fighting?" shrugged S'Ariah.

"Money," said the triceratops. "All she cares about is ticket sales and money."

"Exactly!" said Chloe. "So we're going to make her a business offer that she can't refuse. But we may have to bend the rules a bit…"

Chapter Six.

"Dinosaurs of all species! Citizens of Rextopia! Welcome to... THE GLADIATOR GAMES!"

The Games Master stood in the centre of the arena. Her voice echoed and was joined by a roar unlike any Chloe had ever heard in her life. It was the roar of the T-Rex but, unlike the terrifying sound they made when they ran into battle, this was more of a celebratory cheer. Looking around, she saw the surrounding tyrannosaurs jumping in delight, whooping and screaming. While they looked happy, they still scared the life out of her.

"Ready?" said S'Ariah, leaning over to speak

in her ear. The noise was so loud that they couldn't hear each other even when standing so close. Chloe nodded, but it was a lie.

"Do we have a treat for you lovely people?" boomed the voice of the Games Master. "To start tonight's proceedings, I give you a species of which you have never seen before in the Gladiator Games. Not seen, in fact, since the glory days of the Dino Wars, when the T-Rex army reigned supreme!"

The crowd cheered even louder.

"She knows how to hype up a crowd, I'll give her that," shouted Tuppence.

"A unique fighter, a special guest here in the finest city on New Earth... A HUMAN!"

The crowd went from deafening to silent in seconds. The Games Master flung out her hand and waved at Chloe to join her. Chloe, clinking and clanking with the armour she was wearing, shuffled in to the arena. She felt every pair of eyes on her. Looking at their shocked faces, she could begin to understand their feelings towards her. They would all have lost someone in the Dino Wars, and probably to a human soldier. To hate her was natural. She reached the centre and the Games Master held up her arms and forced her to bow.

"Isn't she marvellous? Humans are known for their trickery and dexterity, but how will she do against her competitor tonight?" called the Games Master. "Let's find out! You know her as a mean, killing machine. Does she still have what it takes? Presenting… Desdemona the Destroyer!"

"GRAAAAHHHH!"

The bellow came from the stands where an albertosaurus, twice the height of Chloe, leapt from the second balcony and into the arena. She was dressed in a helmet and chain mail, holding a machete in each of her short arms.

"Gladiators, READY!" called the Games

Master. "Three… two… one… FIGHT!"

Chloe looked at the puny staff she held in her hands.

"Okay then," she muttered to herself. "This plan better work!"

*

"Typical!" said Adam. "Of all the jobs we could have been picked for, Oska had to sell us to the arena's toilet cleaner!"

The toilets for the Gladiator Games were inside the arena, next to the stairwells. As it was built for T-Rexes, the room was huge and could hold lots of gladiator fans, except that it was like no lavatory Adam had ever been to. T-Rexes didn't seem to think much of privacy, so there were

no cubicles and, as they had yet to work out how to build flushing toilets, there was just a row of buckets up against a wall. Even they seemed to be optional, as occasionally a tyrannosaur would just poop where they stood. Kyle had handed Adam, Benji and Dag a mop and shovel and said: "You'll work out what to do..." before walking away.

"Okay, let's just make sure he's gone before we go and rescue the girls," said Adam. But that was easier said than done. Kyle kept checking on them and whenever they tried to sneak down the corridor, he would sense they were coming and walk towards them. For the time being, they remained inside the bathrooms, emptying dinosaur poo from one bucket to a slightly larger bucket and mopping the floor. After a few hours:

"Dinosaurs of all species! Citizens of Rextopia! Welcome to... THE GLADIATOR GAMES!"

The Games Master's voice could be heard everywhere. It was when she came to mention a human competitor that Dag decided enough was enough.

"Come on," he shouted. He grabbed his mop and bucket of soapy water and ran out through the door. "If we don't act now, Chloe and Tuppence will be human pâté!"

"But–" Adam didn't even get to finish his thought, as Dag ran out of the door. He and Benji shrugged at each other and followed.

"Hey!" came a call from down the corridor. "Where're you going?"

Kyle stood in their way. Adam couldn't see how to get past the large T-Rex, but luckily Dag had always been the creative brain of the group.

"Sorry, Kyle!" said Dag. "I'm on a tea break."

Before Adam could stop him, Dag threw the bucket of water along the length of the corridor. Adam thought he had meant to get Kyle and had missed, but Dag's plan soon became clear.

He ran… and slid down the corridor, using the mop to keep him steady. He zoomed past the confused-looking T-Rexes who were waiting in line to go to the toilet, and saw Kyle coming closer and closer. He picked up his mop and held it out like a knight jousting his opponent.

"Argh!" screamed Kyle as he got the full force of a wet and smelly mop in his face. He fell and Dag leapt over him.

"Come on!" he shouted. Adam and Benji ran to keep up, jumping over poor Kyle. "We've got a gladiator to save!"

*

"Destroy her! Destroy her! Destroy her!" chanted the crowd. The albertosaurus was heavy and slow. That was what provided the entertainment, after all. The crowd loved to see the huge dinosaur galumphing after Chloe, a poor, unskilled fighter. Chloe was succeeding in her plan however – the first part of which was to try and tire out her opponent. She ran back and forth across the arena, never attempting to strike but instead dodging and weaving. She was smaller than the albertosaurus by a long way and so was able to zip around her, duck under her tail and get her out of breath.

The Games Master, sat at the side of the arena, was commentating using a make-shift megaphone, made from an orange plastic cone that humans used to decorate their roads with.

"And she's done it again! The human has dashed through the legs of the challenger. She's small and quick, but will that be enough to win the game?" she said.

Desdemona huffed and puffed.

"Stay still, human!" she said.

"No can do, sorry!" panted Chloe.

She jumped out of the way of Desdemona's swinging tail and ran to the side of the arena, near to where S'Ariah was standing. Chloe caught her eye.

"Now?" said S'Ariah.

"Now!" said Chloe, before running out of the way of the stampeding Desdemona.

Suddenly, S'Ariah opened up her wings, knocking out the two guards that stood either side of her, and took flight to the astonishment of the crowd. She had armed herself with her sling and some rocks from the ground, and spread her wings to hover twenty metres above the arena. She was careful not to go too near to the net, or the guard with the itchy trigger finger.

"Lead her to the middle!" shouted S'Ariah. Chloe ran through the centre of the arena and Desdemona the Destroyer followed. S'Ariah spun the sling and let a hail of stones go, showering the albertosaurus.

"Ow!" she shouted, shocked.

"Goodness!" called the Games Master. "This is unprecedented! Another gladiator has taken to the ring!"

"CHARGE!" called Tuppence. She ran from the side of the arena to the centre, spinning her mace like a true warrior. She brought it down on

Desdemona's tail, causing her to wail in agony.

"And another!" shouted the Games Master. "I don't believe it! Dinos and humans working as one!"

While Desdemona was nursing her tail, Chloe took the chance to bring down her staff on the beast's toes. She cried out again. Chloe couldn't help feeling sorry for the dinosaur, but it was for the good of the mission to save New Earth, she reminded herself.

The Games Master, meanwhile, was speechless; the human girl was only meant to be a quick treat for the crowd, certainly not meant to *win*! She should be calling off the fight, taking the humans and that pterodactyl back to their cell. But she looked at the crowd, laughing and cheering and roaring with delight. They were loving the show! And that was the most important thing, wasn't it? A happy, *paying* audience?

"And so here we have the newest addition to

our happy, Gladiator Games family! I knew you'd love them!" she said. "The Trio of Trouble! The Three Amigos! The *Gladiator Girls*!"

"It's working!" shouted Tuppence to Chloe. "The Games Master is pretending that a tag-team was the plan all along!"

"I knew she would!" called Chloe. "Let's end this!"

S'Ariah continued her barrage of shots from above, a rapid-fire of rocks to keep Desdemona the Destroyer on her toes. Meanwhile, Tuppence and Chloe grabbed a length of rope from the ground that marked the edge of the arena and stretched it out between them.

"CLOTHESLINE!" screamed Tuppence. They ran at their opponent, the rope taut. It hit her legs and within seconds the Destroyer was on the ground, winded and wheezing. Chloe climbed on top of her and the crowd went wild.

"Three… two… one… she's out!" counted the

Games Master over her megaphone. "The Gladiator Girls are the winners!"

S'Ariah landed and took the bows with Tuppence and Chloe, holding hands and rejoicing.

In the crowds, an iguanodon and two humans, who smelt badly of dino-poo, rushed forward to try and catch glimpse of what on earth was going on.

"Come on!" said Dag. "We've got to get down there and save the girls!"

"Alright!" said Adam. "But Chloe is so stubborn that she'd rather fight a T-Rex than get saved by me."

Adam elbowed his way to the front of the crowd and looked down to see his little sister, Tuppence and S'Ariah atop a still dinosaur, bowing and waving to the crowd.

"Dag?" he laughed. "I think they're doing pretty well on their own!"

Chapter Seven.

"That. Was. AMAZING!" yelled Tuppence. Her voice echoed in the dark cell. They were back in their prison underneath the arena, which was eerily quiet after the roar of the crowds above ground. After their victory, they had been handcuffed by Hex and led back down to the cells. Tuppence was only disappointed she didn't get to do a lap of honour.

"What now?" said S'Ariah, also buzzing from their win. "Do we fight again? Should we train some more?"

Chloe sat on the floor, her hands shaking with post-fight nerves.

"Now, we wait," she said. Her plan, so far, had worked. They had defeated Desdemona and they had caught the attention of the Games Master. "Trust me. The Games Master will be down anytime now to make a deal with us."

They waited. Tuppence's adrenaline rush finally wore off and she fell asleep in a corner.

"Anytime… now!" repeated Chloe. "Anytime… NOW!"

But the cells remained silent until she suddenly heard the clink of metal. She turned to the barred window that gave them their only ray of daylight. A shadow was quickly cast over them as a large face appeared there. A large *iguanodon* face...

"Hi Chloe!" came a familiar voice. "We've come to save you!"

Chloe's face fell.

"Dag?" she gasped. "What are you doing here?"

"Saving you!" he said, a big, stupid grin on his

face. He attached a metal hook to the window bars and Chloe heard the clink of chains. "I grabbed these from a store cupboard. I reckon if I make a pulley of some sort and use my strength, I can rip the bars out of here in ten minutes tops."

"But… we don't need saving!" said Chloe. Her eyes flitted back to the corridor. Luckily there was no sign of the Games Master or a guard.

"Told you!" Adam's voice said. He barged Dag out of the way and his face appeared in the window. "Too stubborn to accept our help!"

"I am NOT stubborn!" said Chloe. "Now go away! We've got a plan to get a new Dilotron crystal and get out of here but we can't do it if we get caught with you lot trying to free us."

"Don't worry. I get it!" Adam said. He looked down at Chloe, who looked so strong and grown-up. He was so proud of his little sister that he had to stop himself from grinning. "It'd better work!"

"It will!" said Chloe. "Keep a low profile.

We'll find you when we win the crystal."

"Okey dokey."

Adam reached through the bars and gave her a fist-bump. Chloe smiled, until...

"Why do you smell like dino-poo?" asked Chloe.

"It's a long story," said Adam. "We'd better get out of here. Good luck!"

Adam ducked down and not a moment too soon. A few moments later, Hex brought down a broken and bruised brachiosaurus to their cell, and Leena the mighty T-Rex came strutting back.

"Wonderful show, ladies!" came the Games Master's voice down the stairs. "Bad luck, Desdemona! And you, Mackenzie," she said to the brachiosaurus. "Leena! My grand champion again! You were magnificent!"

"Blimey," whispered Tuppence to Chloe. "I think Leena just blushed!"

The Games Master turned to Hex.

"And as for those three," said the Games Master, her tone lowering, "bring them to my office. NOW."

*

Hex led them in their chains to a plush office at the top of the arena. One side was all glass, looking down on the fighting area where slaves were cleaning up the mess from the nights' entertainment. In the corner of the room was a glass case, where a green Dilotron crystal was displayed, glowing with energy. Sat in a large, leather chair was the Games Master, a tuft of colourful feathers on her head, her feet up on the desk.

"Ladies," she said. "Are you trying to upset me?"

Stood in a line in front of her, Chloe, Tuppence and S'Ariah shook their heads furiously.

"Not at all, Games Master!" S'Ariah said. "We have the greatest respect for you!"

"Then why try to disrupt my games?" she said. Chloe raised her hand.

"Please, Games Master," she said, trying hard to be polite. "We have come very far and we are on a quest. New Earth is in danger. We are travelling to disarm a weapon that could destroy all the dinosaurs on the planet."

"And we need *that*," interrupted Tuppence, pointing to the Dilotron crystal.

The Games Master looked them up and down,

and shrugged.

"And?" she said. "Why should I care?"

She walked over to a hat stand, carefully removed a wig of her colourful feathers from her head and placed it down, leaving her completely bald.

"We'll make a deal," said Chloe. "The next Gladiator Games is tomorrow, yes? Put us on, versus the Grand Champion."

"What?" whispered Tuppence out of the corner of her mouth. "We've only won one match! We can't go up against Leena!?"

"People will want to see the hot new tag-trio go up against the Grand Champion. They'll pay double! You'll be rich!" said Chloe. She had the Games Master's attention. "Think about it – Leena versus the last of the humans! The greatest battle since the Dino Wars!"

"And?" said the bald dinosaur. "What will *you* get?"

"The crystal, and our freedom," she said, putting out her hand to shake. "Then we can go on with our quest, and you'll have enough gold coins to take a bath in."

"And if you lose?"

"It would be an historic victory for all dinos," said Chloe. "And you'll *still* get tonnes of gold!"

Slowly, the Games Master extended a claw. Chloe grabbed it and shook it before S'Ariah or Tuppence could stop her.

"DEAL!"

Chapter Eight.

"Buy your official Gladiator Games T-Shirts here!"

"Barbequed ribs! Freshly killed this morning!!"

"Live snacks! Liver-flavoured popcorn! Fried herbivores! Come and get it!"

The sounds of the street sellers echoed about the outside of the arena, where Adam, Benji and Dag had spent the night sleeping behind some bins. They woke and stretched, but had to scramble and hide when they saw two large T-Rexes who had come to empty the rubbish. The boys squatted in a shadowy doorway and eavesdropped on the bin collectors.

"You going to the Gladiator Games tonight?" said one, a grey-coloured tyrannosaur.

"Of course I am!" said the other, red-scaled T-Rex. "Did you hear about the new team? Two humans and a bird or something?"

"A *pterodactyl*!" muttered Dag under his breath. Adam clamped a hand over his friend's mouth.

"They're taking on the Grand Champion tonight!" said Grey. "Can't wait. Should be a nice little massacre!"

They laughed as they carried the bins away and Adam exchanged a look with Benji.

"So do you still trust Chloe's plan?" asked Benji, picking a chicken bone out of his mass of curly hair.

"Er, yeah. Sure," said Adam, unconvincingly. "But maybe we should go and watch their fight, you know, just in case they need us…"

They peered around a corner to look into the main street, where fans were already gathering for the big fight. Benji looked them all over. It was mostly tyrannosaurs, but other dinosaurs must have come from other cities to watch too. Then he thought he saw someone he knew.

"It's Oska!" said Benji. Sure enough, Oska was stood outside eating a tub of meat-flavoured popcorn. The little lycorhinuses stood beside him. They had even bought little Gladiator Games hats and were jumping up and down, excited for the show. Grak saw Benji peeking around the corner

and they all ran to him, piling on top of him like love-starved puppies.

"BENJI!"

"SO!"

"WORRIED!" said Grak, Trek and Karp.

"TUPPS?" added Hart.

"Missed you too!" said Benji, giving them a squeeze. "Tupps is in there. But don't worry. I think she's going to be fine."

"Oska!" called Adam as the oviraptor walked over to them. "What are you doing here?"

"Adam! Good to see you!" he said. "The whole of the city is here! It was all anyone could talk about in the hotel last night."

"Hotel?"

"Ah, yes! I used the money I made from selling you," he said. "Why, where did you stay last night?"

"Doesn't matter," Adam scowled. "Come this way. We think we've found a service hatch so we can all sneak in to the arena."

Oska took the lead, playing the part of the slave-trader again in case if they came across anyone. They came to a dead end and were about to turn back when Oska held up a claw.

"Well, what do we have here?" he said. Adam wondered what he was talking about, but then spotted it. Suspended on a chain, high above the alley in a metal cage lay a thin-looking dinosaur – with a Stetson hat.

"Klint?" called Adam. The troodon sat up and looked down at them.

"Fellas! Thank the almighty! I thought I'd be up here for ages!" he said, apparently pleased to see them. "The Games Master had me followed and robbed. They stuck me up here for good measure. Y'all couldn't be a sport and let me down, could you?"

Adam, Dag, Oska and Benji looked over at each other, confused.

"No!" said Benji. "You kidnapped my sister, remember?"

"And mine!" said Adam. "And our friend!"

Klint scratched his head. "Are you still sore about that? It's in the past!"

"It was two days ago," said Oska.

"Really? Huh. Time flies," Klint frowned. "Okay. If you let me down, I'll tell you where they are."

"The Gladiator Games?" said Dag. "You already told us."

"Darn it!" the troodon shouted. "Okay, I didn't want to have to do this, but... if you let me down, I'll owe you a..." He could barely bring himself to say the word. "A *favour*!"

Benji couldn't stop himself from laughing.

"Is that it? You take our family and that's all you're offering?" he chuckled.

"Hmm, wait a second," said Oska. "This may be to our advantage. You hippy humans and herbivores may not understand, but to a noble carnivore, a favour is a very powerful thing. After the Dino Wars, we used them as our currency. A favour here, a helping hand there. Before we adopted gold coins as our money, favours were used to build whole cities."

"Can we trust him?" Adam asked Oska.

"As much as any low-life slave trader," he shrugged. "But a favour is an unbreakable bond."

Adam mulled it over.

"You'd owe us a *big* favour," he said. Klint winced.

"Okay! Deal!" he shouted. "Now let me down!"

Adam stood back with his arms crossed.

"Okay," he said. "Grak?"

The tiny lyco nodded and barked orders at his

siblings. When they were alone, Adam had noticed, they would speak in a series of clicks and squawks. Trek ran towards Grak and jumped on his head, Grak flipping him high in the air like a circus acrobat. Trek was flung towards the wall of the nearest building and grabbed hold of a brick with his beak. Karp and Hart followed and Grak climbed on top of Dag to do the same. They used their beaks and claws to scale the wall and leap across to the suspended cage.

"Impressive!" said Klint. "Now how am I meant to get down?"

Karp found a metal hook that secured the chains to the cage and began to peck at it with her chipped tooth.

"HOLD!"

"TIGHT!" said Karp and Hart in turn.

"What? Oh, no!" said Klint, his smile fading.

"OH!"
"YES!" said

Grak and Trek.

One more peck at the hook and the chain came free. As the cage plummeted onto the alley below, the lycorhinuses leapt to safety and climbed

down the walls again. Klint screamed in terror when the cage smashed on the ground, opening and setting him free.

"Yeesh!" he shouted. "You coulda killed me!"

"But we didn't," said Adam. "Now about that

favour..."

Klint sighed and fished around in his pockets, pulling out a small, flat piece of metal. He offered it to Adam.

"It's a whistle," he explained. "Three short blasts and every troodon within a hundred miles will hear it. I'll come find you."

Adam took the whistle and looked it over. He attached it to his belt and clapped his hands, rubbing them together. Klint took off without another word, scurrying down the alley.

"Okay!" he said. "Let's find our seats!"

*

"I've changed my mind!" said Chloe. She paced the floor of their cell, walking two steps forth, two steps back and repeating over and over. "Where's Adam? I'm ready to be rescued now!"

Tuppence had already dressed in her armour ready for the fight. It had gone past dinnertime and they had been treated to a slap-up meal of eggs, pasta, veggies and fruit. Chloe hated being kept prisoner in the cell, but had to admit that she would miss the food when they left.

"Too late," said Tuppence. She had never been very good at reassuring people. "The games start in an hour."

"So… we're stuck," said Chloe.

"Not really!" said S'Ariah, with her always-sunny smile. "We still have the plan!"

The plan. Chloe had arrived back to the cells after they had seen the Games Master and attempted to put together some sort of plan; so far she had come up with 'beat Leena'.

Chloe concentrated on controlling her breathing, calming herself and dressing in armour for the fight. She took her time and then suddenly–

"Gladiator Girls?" called Hex. He gave them a friendly wink. "You're up."

"What? Now?" said Chloe. "We're not ready!"

Hex shrugged.

"I'm not sure that it matters," he said.

He led them up to the arena floor. When they came out into the light, Chloe and Tuppence had to put their fingers in their ears to block out the unbelievable noise. S'Ariah put her talons over the holes where her ears would have been, if she had had ears.

Chloe turned to say something to her friends, but it was useless trying to talk over the noise. On the other side of the arena was a small podium where the Games Master stood with her megaphone. Behind her stood the glass case with the green Dilotron crystal and in front of her stood a large bag of gold coins. The Games Master caught Chloe's eye and smiled. She pointed to the sack of gold and winked, as if to say 'Thanks for all the ticket sales!'

"Ladies and gentlemen! Tyrannosaurs of all shapes and sizes! Fellow carnivores and even disgusting herbivores! Welcome to the Gladiator Games Grand Champion Show Down!" the Games Master announced. The crowd went crazy, cheering like it was their last chance to watch the games and have some fun (which, Chloe reminded herself, it might be if they didn't continue on the quest quickly).

"Here we go!" Tuppence said, jumping up and down with either excitement or fear.

"They made a name for themselves last night in the Gladiator Games hall of fame. They are the next generation of fighters, a force to be reckoned with – give it up for the Gladiator Girls!"

The crowd cheered again and they stepped into the middle of the arena, waving to the audience. S'Ariah twirled her sling, and Chloe raised her staff up to a chorus of cheers, Tuppence even blew some kisses.

"And defending her title... she needs no introduction... welcome Rextopia's own Grand Champion... Leena!"

Leena stomped into the arena, armoured and holding a mighty broadsword. She let out a bone-chilling roar that sent a bolt of fear down Chloe's spine. The crowd roared back, showing their love for their champion.

They faced off in the centre of the arena.

"Hey, if I rip you to shreds, it's nothing personal," said Leena with a sneer.

"Yeah, well..." Tuppence struggled to come up with some trash talk. "Don't take it too hard if we... um... break your tiny arms!"

"Let's get ready to rumble!" said the Games Master from her podium. "As you know, the prize for defeating the champion is freedom and the Emerald Gem! No one has managed it yet, but can the Gladiator Girls do it?"

A chorus of boos came from the crowd.

"Hey, I thought *some* of them might be on our side..." sulked Tuppence.

At that point, Adam, Dag and Benji managed to creep through the crowd, having entered through a service door that dinosaurs used to deliver food. They avoided the toilets where Kyle would be on the warpath for them, and even managed to squeeze into the ring-side area near to the Games Master's podium.

"We're not too late," said Dag. "Look, there are the girls."

"And there's the Dilotron crystal," said Adam, looking over at the podium.

"So let's get to it!" yelled the Games Master. "Usual Grand Champion Show Down rules apply. On my signal, you will fight... to the DEATH!"

Chapter Nine.

Chloe looked over to the Games Master, her eyes wide with panic.

"WHAT?" she screamed. "You never told us that!"

The Games Master grinned and shrugged.

"Remember, dear spectators, you decide who lives and dies in this battle. When one contender is on the ground, you will vote if they deserve to die by the hand of their opponent."

Tuppence gulped.

"Did she say... the 'D' word?" she asked. "Awesome plan, Chloe."

"THREE..." the Games Master chanted.

The crowd joined in.

Chloe gripped her staff.

"TWO…"

Tuppence and S'Ariah put on their 'mean' faces, glowering at Leena.

"ONE…"

Adam and Dag glanced at one another, praying Chloe's plan would pay off.

"FIGHT!"

S'Ariah immediately took flight, spinning her sling again. Tuppence and Chloe spread out, figuring that Leena couldn't fight both of them at once. Leena instinctively followed Tuppence, trying to defeat the smallest of them first.

"Strike, Chloe!" called Dag from the side.

"GO!"

"TUPPS!"

"GO!"

"TUPPS!" shouted Grak, Trek, Karp and Hart in turn.

S'Ariah pelted Leena with a handful of rocks from her sling, but this time it did little to distract her from her target, Tuppence. She swooped down low, trying to pelt her from behind but Leena's concentration was immovable. S'Ariah got too close however and Leena's long tail clipped the bag of ammunition, ripping it and sending the rocks scattering over the arena. While she hovered in the air, S'Ariah reached down to her belt for more ammunition but found none. It was empty! She spotted some rocks she could use on the ground below her and dived, scooping them up as she glided less than a metre from the ground.

It was the opportunity that Leena needed – she galloped over and thrashed her tail in S'Ariah's direction, bashing her out of the air as easy as if she had swatted a fly. The crowd cheered as

S'Ariah was thrown from the arena and landed in the audience, her sling falling to the ground.

"And one is down already! Rules state that gladiators must stay in the arena. The flying dino is out of the fight!" The Games Master called.

While Leena was busy celebrating her win, Tuppence had taken the chance to run at her from behind. She used her sloping tail as a ramp and ran up, landing squarely on her back, between her shoulder blades.

"Gah!" cried Leena. "Get off me you filthy human!"

"No way, champ!" said Tuppence. She held on tight and kicked as hard as she could, but she barely made a bruise on Leena. The tyrannosaur leapt and ran, trying to throw the six-year-old from her like a bucking bronco. The crowd laughed, loving the new move.

"HOLD ON!" screamed Benji as Tuppence passed them.

"Thanks!" shouted Tuppence. "I hadn't thought of that!"

Leena leapt around the arena and Tuppence had an idea. If she could use her mace to bash Leena on the head, the beast could drop down, unconscious. She looked at her belt where the mace was wedged. To grab it meant taking a hand off the dinosaur's hide. It was her only chance. She quickly let go and reached for her weapon–

And Leena flung her off. Tuppence somersaulted in the air and landed face down in the dirt and sawdust of the arena floor, her mace clattering down next to her. She hit her head and blacked out.

"Another one bites the dust!" called the Games Master. "Just one human left! Remember – the game isn't over until one of the opponents kicks the bucket!"

Chloe didn't need reminding. She looked over, her bottom lip quivering with nerves. She had to do something!

Adam, watching from the sidelines, saw her pause. She was frightened. He wanted to leap in and help her, but the guards would stop him. What would get her pumped up? What would get her angry enough to fight a T-Rex? Suddenly he knew. He fought his way closer to her.

Chloe ran around the outside of the arena, eager to get away from Leena, but she needn't have worried – the Grand Champion was too busy strutting up and down for the crowd, taking bows for ousting Tuppence.

"Hey!" came a call from the stands. "How's the plan going?"

Chloe turned.

"Adam!" she shouted. "We have to go! It's all gone wrong!"

Adam pushed his way to the front and smiled.

"Just remember to keep your guard up. Try to go for the chin!"

"What?" said Chloe. "Are you honestly giving me fighting tips?"

"Of course," he shrugged. "I'm the best fighter in the family, after all."

Chloe gritted her teeth and gripped her weapon tighter.

Adam locked eyes with her.

"Maybe I should take your place," he said. "After all, you're just my little sister tagging along, right?"

Chloe slammed her staff on the ground and pulled herself up to her full height. Adam smiled. He knew how to get her angry, and that was just what she needed at that moment. She turned back to the arena and stomped into the centre.

"Hey! Meat-breath!" she shouted. "The game isn't over yet!"

"Ha!" yelled Leena. "It soon will be!"

She swung her broadsword at Chloe who was quick on her feet. She leapt over the blade as it whooshed beneath her and threw herself out of the way. She got back to her feet and ran to the far side of the arena.

"And the human is on the run! Looks like the Grand Champion will be victorious again!"

But Chloe – finally – had a plan. She had spied S'Ariah's sling abandoned on the ground and picked it up. Arming it with some rocks and dust from the floor, she began to spin it. She only needed one shot – which was lucky, because that was all she had.

"Stop running away, human!" bellowed Leena. "Come and fight like a real woman!"

Spin-spin-spin… She picked up the speed and let the sling go, throwing it at her enemy. The rocks from the floor were soft and chalky, which was good for Chloe. They struck their target and burst apart as they hit Leena square on the nose. The rock turned to powder and fogged up her eyes, stinging them and blinding her temporarily.

"Yes!" cheered Dag. "Go for it, Chloe!"

Chloe ran to Tuppence, who still lay on the floor in a daze. She grabbed the mace at her side and ran back towards Leena, who was thrashing and wailing.

"Looks like our plucky human has a plan!" called the Games Master.

Chloe stood in front of the T-Rex, blinking and blind. She felt kind of sorry for Leena – her arms were so short she couldn't even rub her eyes. But there was no room for pity in the world of a gladiator. Chloe spun the heavy mace and brought it down hard on Leena's foot. There was a loud crunch and Leena leapt onto one foot, roaring with pain.

Chloe smiled. It was working. She knew that she couldn't beat a large dinosaur like Leena, but the great thing about two-legged creatures like tyrannosaurs was that once they were down to one leg, they tipped over easily…

She swung her staff at Leena's ankle and pushed hard to unbalance her.

"Woooooooooah!" shouted the crowd as Leena toppled down. She crashed down in a cloud of dust. She had knocked the breath out of herself and was unable to get up. Chloe climbed on top of her.

"The Grand Champion has been toppled!" came the Games Master's voice through the megaphone. "But the game is not over. Gracious fans, do you want our new champion to end Leena's life? Stand for yes, sit for no!"

Chloe looked around the audience.

Each tyrannosaur, with no exception, stood.

Carnivores, she thought. *Of course they want blood.*

"Do it," groaned Leena.

But Chloe was exhausted, and certainly no killer. She leapt down from atop Leena and climbed instead onto the podium next to the Games Master.

"If you do not finish the fight, you do not win," the Games Master said. She produced her sharp, bone-handled knife. "Here, take this and claim your freedom."

Chloe looked down at the knife and shook her head. Instead, she took the Games Master's place at the podium. The audience was silent, eager to

see what the crazy human would do next. Chloe looked up and called out to the stadium full of fans.

"I won't kill," she shouted. The T-Rexes surrounding her murmured. "I know that will come as a shock to you, as carnivores, but I am here for a bigger purpose. I came to Rextopia looking for one thing: the Emerald Gem. My friends and I are on a mission to save dinosaurs from extinction and we need this crystal. If we do not have it, in less than two weeks you will all perish. We asked the Games Master for it, but she refused, saying we had to fight for it. Well, now I have, and I have won it. So if you think I should walk away with this crystal to save New Earth, sit down for peace. I trust you will, because I know tyrannosaurs are noble dinosaurs."

She let her words echo around the arena, and waited. For a moment, the tyrannosaurs stood still, looking to each other in confusion. Then, one by one, they began to sit. They sat silently and Chloe breathed a sigh of relief. Adam, Dag and Benji leapt the barrier to join her, followed by Oska and the lycorhinuses.

"Hand over the crystal, Games Master," said Adam.

The Games Master stood, frowning. She folded her arms and refused to meet his eye.

"You had to earn it!" she protested. But then the sound of huffing and puffing came from the arena. Leena limped up to the podium, bleeding from her head. She stomped up and raised her broadsword in her hand and swung.

Chloe ducked–

And heard the sound of a glass cabinet shattering. She looked up and saw Leena plucking the green crystal from its stand. She held it out for Chloe, who took it gratefully.

"Get out of here," she growled, smiling. "You've got a mission to complete."

Chapter Ten.

The streets of Rextopia were full of T-Rexes filing out from the arena. They were excited when they saw the Gladiator Girls standing outside; some even asked for autographs.

"Great fight!" said one infant tyrannosaur. She had a bow on her head and held out a book with her stubby arms for Chloe to sign. "Pity you'll be free now. Come back and be a full-time gladiator!"

Chloe laughed and signed the book. Adam appeared behind her and tapped her on the shoulder. She turned and her face hardened.

"Oh, it's you!" she said. "Hey, who's the best

fighter in the family now, huh?"

Adam just stood and smiled.

"What?" said Chloe. "Back in the arena, remember? You said that you were the best fighter? Agh, it got me so angry! I–" she paused. Adam continued to smile smugly. "You… you did it on purpose! You got me angry so I'd fight Leena! You complete and utter total bag of dino droppings!"

She hit him playfully on the arm, while Adam burst into laughter.

"It worked though, didn't it?" he said, in between punches.

Dag returned from a back street where they had stored some of their kit while they watched the games. He held out a bag and opened the top. A strange, rainbow glow came from within.

"Here they are," he said. "The other Dilotron crystals."

"And we finally have the fourth!" said

S'Ariah, holding the green crystal aloft. She went to put it in the bag, but the other stones glowed so bright that she took it away again. "I'll keep it safe. We don't want them exploding with energy before we need to disarm the Coda Program."

Adam put his hand behind his back.

"What have you got there?" asked Chloe. "You're doing that weird thing with your mouth again."

"I'm smiling!" he laughed. "I wanted to get you something for becoming Grand Champion. I knew you'd have to give up the crystal, so..."

He presented Chloe with a metal pendant, the very same one he had found on the back-alley market stall.

"This is from Bastion!" Chloe gasped. "How did you get it?"

"I used the rest of the money from Oska selling us as slaves," said Adam. "Then I rushed back to the market after the games and haggled. A lot!"

"But if this is from Bastion, how–?"

"No idea," said Adam. "I'm pretty sure it was made by Mum though."

Speechless, Chloe hugged her brother.

Tuppence, a bandage wrapped around her head, saw Benji through the crowds and ran to hug him.

"I never thought I'd be happy to see you again!" she said. Then: "Ugh! Why do you smell like a rubbish dump?"

"No reason…" said Benji. Oska and the lycorhinuses exited the arena, leaping over excitedly to see the twins.

"Well done all!" said Oska. "But I think we should be pressing on. By my count, we only have ten days left to get to the laboratory."

They all nodded. Exhausted, they began to walk through the crowds towards the city walls.

"Oi!" came a call.

It was Leena. She looked a little battered and

bruised, but still as mighty and scary as ever. She stomped through the crowd.

Leena leaned forward and Chloe tensed, fully expecting to be torn limb from limb. But the Grand Champion simply spread her small arms and hugged Chloe.

"Best fight I've had in years!" she said. "Most of 'em just give up and let me beat 'em. You put up a real battle!"

"Aw, thanks!" said Chloe. "It was a pleasure to fight you, Grand Champion!"

Leena looked down.

"Yeah, except I'm not, am I? Champion, that is..." she sulked. "You beat me. And the Games Master threw me out of my cell. She told me never to come back!"

Dag nervously stepped forwards.

"B-but if Chloe didn't finish the fight by killing you, she isn't the champion, is she?" he stuttered.

"You still have the title."

Leena perked up.

"And... if you're not in the cells, that means you're free, doesn't it?" said Adam. "You're not a slave anymore!"

Chloe gave Leena a friendly punch on the arm.

"Looks like you have a life to live, Leena," she smiled. She couldn't be sure, but she could have sworn Leena was crying tears of joy.

"Get out of Rextopia!" she roared. "Never let me see you around here again! And... good luck. Save us all."

They walked to the city gates, where the guards had heard about their quest, and had been given orders from their bosses to let them out.

"We entered as slaves, but left as heroes!" said Adam.

"As thieves, more like!" said a voice from behind them. They turned to see the Games Master walking towards them, her wig askew.

"You took my gem! What am I going to do for a prize now?"

"Oh, hush!" said Chloe. "We'll bring it back once we're finished with it!"

The Games Master stopped.

"Oh really?" she said. "We'll see – I can't see a group of herbivores and their pet humans lasting long. There's far worse than T-rex's out there. Either way... I'll be waiting."

The guards opened the gates and the motley bunch of dinosaurs and humans walked back out into the scrublands. Adam held out his hand to Chloe.

"Map?" he barked. "Or are you too good for that now, Miss High-And-Mighty Gladiator?" he grinned.

"It's fine, I'll read the map," she said, pulling it out of her bag. "But if there are any fearsome carnivores that need tackling, you can leave that to me now..."

They stepped away from the gates and the guards slowly began to close them.

"It's funny, really," called the Games Master. The gates were about to close when she added: "You're the second human to come asking for that green crystal."

SLAM!

The gates closed, leaving Adam and Chloe staring at where the Games Master had been, their mouths wide open.

"*Second* human?" said Adam. "But… the only other humans are back in Bastion... aren't they?"

He stared at his sister and the twins in disbelief for a few moments.

"Do you think that's how the pendant ended up in Rextopia?" he asked.

"Maybe… somewhere out there… there are more of us?" said Chloe. "And if so..."

"We wouldn't be alone any more."

Slowly, their heads spinning with new

information, Chloe and Adam stepped forwards onto the final leg of their journey, into unknown lands and unknown challenges.

DISCUSSION POINTS

In *Dino Wars: The Gladiator Games,* the main characters are faced with **SEPARATION** for the first time.
- How do each of the characters deal with being split into two groups?
- What do the characters learn from this experience?
- Which perspectives do we see because of this separation?

Chloe struggles with her **SELF CONFIDENCE** in the book.
- How does she overcome the challenges she faces through learning to be confident?
- Why is self-confidence important?
- Where does Chloe's self-importance grow from? What skills does she learn?

Throughout the *Dino Wars* series, there is an underlying theme of **TOLERANCE**.
- How do different characters in *Dino Wars: The Gladiator Games* show tolerance to other people

and species?
- Which moments highlight the divisions between groups of people and dinosaurs? How do the characters overcome this intolerence?
- Why do you think Adam and his group are tolerant?

When both groups are in sticky situations, they learn to be **RESOURCEFUL**. This means they think on their feet.
- Where in the story does this help the characters break out of their difficult situation?
- How are the characters resourceful in different ways?
- Why is it important to be resourceful?

REVIEWS of DINO WARS

"The story is filled with **ACTION** and **ADVENTURE**, which will have your jaw on the ground. I couldn't stop thinking about what'll happen next!"
Year 5 student at Anglesey Primary School, Birmingham

"Dinos, Dilotron crystals and computer chaos - a raptor **ROLLERCOASTER** for all young action fans!"
Claire Barker, author of the *Knitbone Pepper* series

"This **CAPTIVATING** story manages to incorporate everything that you would want to read in an adventure."
Landscore Primary School, Crediton, Devon

★★★★★
"If you have children that **LOVE** dinosaurs and adventure, then order a copy today! I'm sure they won't be disappointed."
What's Good to Read

"A **QUICK** and **ACTION-PACKED** read [...] This early chapter book is a good choice for dinosaur fans who enjoy action and adventure."
Books for Topics

"I **CAN'T WAIT** to hear how their crystal mission continues [...] More, please!"
Clare Elsom, author and illustrator of *Horace & Harriet*